to Victoria Chess

ANNIE and the

Library of Congress Cataloging in Publication Data
Gackenbach, Dick. Annie and the Mud Monster.
Summary: Annie goes to a costume party dressed as a
potato, but something is not quite right with her cos-
tume. Then a Mud Monster helps her out with her prob-
lem. [1. Mud—Fiction. 2. Costume—Fiction] I. Title.
PZ7.G 117An   [E]   81-8344
ISBN 0-688-00791-0   AACR2
ISBN 0-688-00792-9 (lib. bdg.)

MUD MONSTER

Dick Gackenbach

Lothrop, Lee & Shepard Books • New York

One day I was invited to a costume party.
"Come dressed as a vegetable," I was told.
So I decided to go as a potato.
"Will you please help me make a potato?"
I asked my mother.
"Yes, I will," she said.

My mother and I made a potato with wire and cloth, and with brown buttons for eyes.

When we were finished, my mother was pleased. "You should win first prize for the best costume," she said.

"Maybe so," I replied, "but I think there's something missing from my potato."

"What could that be?" my mother wanted to know.

"I don't know," I said. "I will have to think about it."

That's just what I was thinking about
as I walked to the party. "Now what does this
potato need?" I wondered.

Suddenly, out of nowhere, I heard a voice.
"I know what's wrong with that potato, kid," it said.
I turned around, but no one was there.

Then I heard the voice again.
"That is the worst potato I've ever seen."

It sounded to me like the voice was coming
out of a mud puddle.

I got down on my knees to have a look.

"As a potato, kid," the voice boomed, "you
make a better tomato."

The puddle began to ripple and bubble
like a pot of boiling soup.

Now I was sure the voice was coming
from the mud.

Just as I thought that,
I saw an eye pop out of the mud puddle.
Then, another eye.

Then, a head.

Before I knew it, a Mud Monster was standing over me, all dirty and dripping mud.

"Kid," the Monster said, "don't you know there's no such thing as a *clean* potato?"

"My mother has clean potatoes," I told him.

"That's because mothers and fathers wash potatoes the minute they get their hands on them. But take my word for it," he said, "potatoes come out of the ground covered with dirt."

"Well," I had to admit, "I thought something was missing from my potato."

"You bet there is!" he said. "And dirt is what that potato needs."

"Are you sure?" I asked.

"Of course I'm sure!" he screamed. "Does it snow in Alaska? Trust me, pal. Potatoes should be dirty. Now, do you want to win first prize, or don't you?" he demanded to know.

"Yes," I said. "I want to win."

"Well then," the Mud Monster warned, "you'd better listen to me and mess up that potato."

I sat down and thought it over.

Surely, I thought, he should know what he's talking about. A Mud Monster should know everything there is to know about a potato. After all, he is made of dirt.

Finally, I made up my mind.

"Okay," I said. "What do I have to do to be a perfect potato and win a prize?"

"Good girl!" he cried.

Then he took my hand and pulled me into the puddle.
Together, we danced and jumped and slid
and had a wonderful time.
When we stopped, I was covered with mud.

"Now," Mud said with a smile,
"that's what I call a great potato."
"Me too," I said.
I was happy with my potato at last!
"Thanks," I told Mud, and went on to the party.

When I got to the party,
I met a carrot and a pepper.
"Wow," Carrot said to me.
"I never saw anything so dirty."
"Ugh, muddy Potato,"
said Pepper. "Stay
away from me."

I tried to be careful at the party, but I made a mess wherever I went.

I dropped mud in the party punch, and all over the chocolate cake.

I got mud on the onion, and smeared the cucumber, and smudged mud on the tomato too.

After that, all the vegetables got together and turned the garden hose on me.

"Who wants a dirty potato at a party?" they said.

The water from the hose made the lawn very wet, and soon it was full of mud.

"Ha!" I said. "Serves you right. Now the Mud Monster's got you!" Then I left the party.

"Nobody knows a good potato when they see one," I let them know.

When I got home, I told my mother what had happened, and all about the Mud Monster.

"There's no such thing," she told me. "You just wanted to play in the mud. Anyway," she said, "muddy or not, you're first prize with me."

Then she gave me a big kiss, and that was better than any prize I could have won at any party.